ELMER-AGAIN

D0316562

For Angelo and Laura

**MORAY COUNCIL
LIBRARIES &
INFO.SERVICES**

20 20 60 22

Askews

JA

A Red Fox Book

Published by Random House Children's Books, 61-63 Uxbridge Road, London W5 5SA

A division of Random House UK Ltd., London, Melbourne, Sydney, Auckland, Johannesburg and agencies throughout the world

First published by Andersen Press Limited 1991. Red Fox edition 1992. © David McKee 1991

17 19 20 18 16

The right of David McKee to be identified as the author of this work has been asserted by him in accordance with the Copyright, Designs and Patents Act 1988.

This book is sold subject to the condition that it shall not, by way of trade or otherwise, be lent, resold, hired out, or otherwise circulated without the publisher's prior consent in any form of binding or cover other than that in which it is published and without a similar condition including this condition being imposed on the subsequent purchaser.

Printed in China

ISBN 978 0 099 91720 5 (from January 2007)
ISBN 0 09 991720 3

ELMER AGAIN

David McKee

FOX RED

Elmer, the patchwork elephant, was bored. It was two days before another Elmer's day parade – the day when elephants cover themselves with bright patterns. The colours were ready and the elephants were quietly thinking about how they would decorate themselves.

Elmer didn't have to think. He was always coloured grey for the parade, the only grey elephant.

"Time for a walk," he said to himself.

As he walked Elmer thought, "It's too quiet around here. We need a joke or something to liven things up." He came to a pool and looked at his reflection.

"Hello Elmer," he said to himself in the water. "You've just given me a good idea. Thank you."

When he returned the others were still quietly thinking. Elmer went up to one of them and whispered in his ear. The other elephant smiled and winked but said nothing. Elmer settled down for a rest. He had a long night in front of him.

When night fell Elmer waited until the others were asleep.
Then, taking care not to wake them, he set to work.

Before sunrise he had finished and he tiptoed off to another part of the forest to sleep for what was left of the night.

In the morning the first elephant to wake looked at his neighbour and said, "Good morning Elmer."

One after another the elephants woke, and as they did, from every direction came, "Good morning Elmer," "GOOD morning Elmer," "Good MORNING Elmer," "GOOD MORNING Elmer," "Good Morning ELMER," and so on.

During the night Elmer had painted all the elephants to look like him. Now there were Elmers everywhere and nobody knew which was the real one.

Then the elephants started to speak to each other and say things like, "Are you Elmer?"

"I don't know," the other might say. "I might be today, but I'm sure I wasn't yesterday."

Then, one of the elephants called out, "This is another Elmer trick. Come on. Let's splash across the river and wash off the colours. Then we'll see who the real Elmer is."

The elephants raced to the river and splashed and sploshed their way to the other side.

Once on the other side the elephants
stared. They were *all* grey.

"Where's Elmer?" they asked.

"Here of course," said a grey elephant.
"Don't you recognise me?"

"But you're the same colour as us,"
gasped the others.

"So I am," said Elmer. "Wonderful. I
always wanted to be like you."

"This is awful," said another elephant.
"Elmer can't be like the rest of us. Things
won't be the same without an Elmer."

"Well there's nothing I can do about it," said Elmer, "unless . . ."

"What?" said the others.

"Well," said Elmer, "the colours that washed off are still floating on the water. Perhaps if I run back through them I may return to normal."

"Try it," shouted the others. "Try anything to get your colours back."

"Yahoo!" called Elmer, and he raced across the river and vanished into the trees on the other side.

Almost at once he reappeared puffing and panting, but once again in his bright patchwork colours.

"Hurrah!" cheered the elephants from acrosss the river. "It worked. We've got our Elmer again." With that the elephants started chanting, "ELMER, ELMER, ELMER."

Beside Elmer another elephant suddenly appeared from out of the trees. "Did you call?" he asked. The other elephants went silent and stared. This other elephant was soaking wet as if he had just run across the river. On top of that both Elmer and the other elephant were laughing.

"You tricked us," said one elephant to the wet, grey elephant. "You were working with Elmer and pretended to be him. We should have known Elmer's colours wouldn't wash off. It's another Elmer trick."